Goofy and the Enchanted Castle

Random House 🏠 New York

Book Club Edition

First American Edition. Copyright © 1980 by Walt Disney Productions. All rights reserved under International and Pan-American Copyright Conventions. Published in the United States by Random House, Inc., New York, and simultaneously in Canada by Random House of Canada Limited, Toronto. Originally published in Denmark as FEDTMULE OG DET FORHEKSEDE SLOT by Gutenberghus Gruppen, Copenhagen. ISBN: 0-394-84805-5   Manufactured in the United States of America
A B C D E F G H I J K   1 2 3 4 5 6 7 8 9 0

Once there was a king who had
two sons, Harold and Gerald.
They were always showing off.
Each one wanted to be a hero.

One day the two brothers decided
to look for adventure.

On that same day, a simple fellow named
Goofy also set out.

But Goofy was not looking for adventure.
He just wanted to take a quiet walk
in the woods.

By and by the two brothers met Goofy.
"Come with us," said Harold.
The two brothers looked very mean.
Goofy was afraid to say no.
So he went with them into the woods.

By and by they came to an ant hill.
"Watch this!" said Harold.

He began to poke the ant hill.
The ants came running out.

"Stop!" cried
Goofy. "I like ants!"
So the brother
left the ants alone.

By and by they came to a lake.
A duck was standing on a rock.
"Watch this!" said Gerald.
He started to shoot the duck.
"Stop!" said Goofy. "Be kind to ducks!"
So the brother left the duck alone.

By and by they came to a bee hive.

Once more the brothers thought they would have some fun.

They began to shake the bee hive.

"Stop!" cried Goofy. "Bees are my friends too!"

So Harold and Gerald left the bees alone.

Finally they came
to an old castle.

"Let us see who
lives there," said
the brothers.

First Harold knocked at the door.
There was no answer.
Then Gerald pushed the door open
and called out.
Still there was no answer.

But when they walked inside,
they saw something amazing.
They saw people having dinner.

But the people were made of stone!

"This castle must be under a
terrible spell," said Harold.

"I'm going home!" said Goofy.
"No you're not!" said Gerald.

They went into another room.
There they met a little man.
"You are right," he said. "This castle
is under a spell. Whoever breaks the spell
will be a hero."

"I will break the
spell!" cried Harold.
"Good," said the
little man. "Bring me
the one thousand pearls that
are lost in the woods."

The next morning Harold went into
the woods.

He searched all day for the pearls.
But he did not find even one.

So Harold went back
to the castle.

"Finding those pearls
is impossible!" he told
the little man.

"Nothing is impossible!"
said the little man.

And then Harold
turned to stone.

"Surely you can break the spell," said
the little man to Gerald. "Just bring me
the golden key. It lies at the bottom
of the lake."

So Gerald went to the lake.
He dove into the water.

He swam to the very bottom.
There he looked for the golden key.
But he could not find it.

At last Gerald went back to the castle. "Finding a tiny key at the bottom of a big lake is impossible," he told the little man.

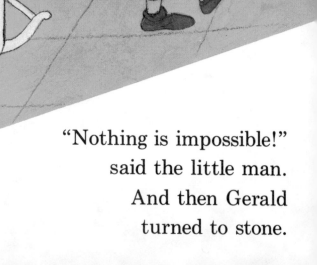

"Nothing is impossible!" said the little man. And then Gerald turned to stone.

Goofy had seen enough!

He decided to leave
right away.
Then he heard the
little man's voice.

"Now it is your turn to try to break
the spell!" said the little man.

"I don't want a turn!" said Goofy.
"Somebody else can have my turn."

"You must try!" said the little man.

So Goofy went into the woods.
He looked everywhere for the pearls.

But all he found were trees and rocks!

Goofy sat down to rest.

Soon he saw some ants marching toward him.

"You saved our ant hill," said the ants. "So now we will save you."

Suddenly Goofy saw a long line of ants.
Each ant was carrying a pearl!
Goofy put the pearls in a bag and
ran back to
the castle.

"Here are all the pearls that were lost
in the woods!" Goofy said proudly.
   "Good!" said the little man
when he saw the sack of pearls.

"But now you must bring me the golden key
that lies at the bottom of the lake," he
said to Goofy.

Golly, thought Goofy.
I don't even know how
to swim.

When Goofy got to the
lake he didn't know what to do.
Then a duck swam up to him.
"You once saved my life,"
said the duck. "So now I
will save yours."

"How can you
save my life?"
asked Goofy.

"Watch this!" said the duck.
And she dove into the water.

The duck swam far down to the
very bottom of the lake.

And she came up with the key!
"Oh, thank you!" said Goofy.

So Goofy went back to the castle.
"Here is the golden key," said Goofy.

"May I go now?"
"No," said the little man. "There is
one more job to do."

The little man showed Goofy a beautiful
flower garden.

"Here is your last job," he said. "Bring
me the sweetest flower in this garden."

Goofy began to smell the flowers.
Every flower smelled just as sweet
as the last.

"This job is impossible!" he said.

Just then he heard a buzzing sound.
Goofy looked up and saw a Queen Bee.

"I came to thank you for saving my
hive," she said. "And I came to help you."
"How can you help me?" asked Goofy.
"Watch this!" said the Queen Bee.

Off she flew to taste
the nectar of every
flower in the garden.

Delicious! Scrumptious!
At last she showed Goofy the sweetest
flower of them all.

Goofy took the flower
to the little man.

"Goofy," he said, "I knew
you could do it!"

In his place stood a tall and happy king.
"Long ago a terrible witch put a spell
on my castle," said the king. "She said
the spell would end only when I found
someone to do the impossible three times."

"And Goofy," said the king, "You did it!"

Everyone in the castle
came back to life.
Harold and Gerald, too!
The king gave each
brother a bag of gold
and sent them away.

But Goofy stayed with the king in his castle.
One night at dinner the king asked Goofy,
"How did you do it? Tell me how you did the
impossible three times."

"It was easy," said Goofy. "I did it
with a little help from my friends."